Brutus Loses His Sniffer

Dyslexic Friendly Edition

TIF E. BOOTS

Illustrated by Syranity Barker

ShelteringTree.Earth, LLC PO Box 973, Eagle Lake, FL 33839 ShelteringTreeMedia.com

What is a "Dyslexic Friendly" Book?

Sheltering Tree Media has taken steps to make our books more friendly for those who live with dyslexia. While the following principles will not make every book readable for every reader, it is our best effort to create products that encourage reading and to support all readers.

Throughout the book, we use a font named OpenDyslexic. This is a free font that is designed to help dyslexic readers distinguish each letter from the others. For more information about OpenDyslexic, how it differs from other fonts, and research behind the font, visit their website: www.opendyslexic.com.

In our books created for children, we use a font size which provides the reader with plenty of spacing between the letters (which is called *kerning*). The bigger, wider font tends to be easier to the reader's eyes.

The space between each word is increased (this is called *word spacing*). This helps better to distinguish when one word ends and the next begins. The line spacing is greater than most common fonts (this is called *leading*). This all should help with readability.

Whenever possible, the text is Left-Aligned but it is not justified on the right side. Allowing the right side of a paragraph to remain *rough* keeps the word spacing consistent throughout.

Our Dyslexic Friendly books are printed on cream or ivory paper which is also thicker than the average book page. This minimizes the sharp contrast of black-on-white pages as well as bleedthrough of text from the previous page.

Finally, Sheltering Tree Media has made colored overlays available when you purchase a book through our online store. You can find these overlays at ShelteringTreeMedia.com/shop/dyslexic-friendly.

These are some of the principles we use to create a book as readable as possible to those living with dyslexia. Some may find this helpful; some may not. Please provide us with any insights you might have to improve our Dyslexic Friendly principles. We pray this will enable many to heighten their love for reading.

DEDICATION

To all the children
who have found joy in
the friendships and
adventures that Brutus
and Scrump share.

It was a clear and sunny day and Scrump was enjoying the dappled sunshine at the edge of the clover field. He was happy to munch on the pale purple flowers that bloomed in the sea of green. As he ate, he heard a faint sound behind him. His body stiffened - ready to run.

"Hey Scrump," Brutus yelled from across the field. "Do you want to play hide and seek today?" Scrump relaxed when he heard Brutus' voice. There was no reason to run away from Brutus. Brutus may have been a puppy, but he was Scrump's best friend.

Brutus Loses His Sniffer

"That sounds fun, but where is Charlie today?" Scrump was referring to the Grey squirrel who was usually with them. "I'm not sure," said Brutus. "I haven't seen him yet today." "Let's go find him and see if he wants to play before we start a game," suggested Scrump. "Ok," said Brutus. "I do not want him to feel left out if he can play today."

Scrump and Brutus walked out of the clover field together and made their way to the fence around the pond. They called for Charlie but did not go on the pond side of the fence. Charlie did not call back so they continued to walk to the garden. They searched up and down rows and rows of vegetables and berries.

They did not see Charlie in the vegetable garden but they found Dash holding his basket while his human harvested tomatoes. Scrump quickly hid in the shadows of leafy plants while Brutus greeted Dash.

"Good morning, Dash. We are looking for Charlie to see if he wants to play today. Have you seen him?"

"I have not seen him for a couple of days. I sure hope he is not stuck in a tree again." Dash chuckled.

"Me too, I do not want to have to get him down again." Brutus laughed. "If you see him, will you tell him we are looking for him?"

"Will do," agreed Dash as his human reached back to put another tomato in his basket.

From the garden they went to the flower beds, then to the playground. Charlie wasn't at either spot. "Where should we look next?" asked Scrump. "Sometimes my owner puts out nuts and seeds on the porch for the birds. Maybe Charlie is there," suggested Brutus. "That's a good idea," agreed Scrump and they walked toward the back porch.

They looked all around and under the back porch. Still, they could not find Charlie. After climbing the stairs to look on the back porch, they found the fat orange cat sleeping on the railing in the sun.

"I think the cat never leaves this spot," whispered Scrump.

Brutus nodded then interrupted the cat's nap. "Excuse me, Mrs. Cat. I'm sorry to disturb you again. We are looking for our friend Charlie to see if he wants to play hide and seek. We have already checked the pond and garden, as well as the flower beds and playground."

"Have you seen him?" asked Scrump.

"Well," said the cat with a yawn. "I would say that you guys have done a good job seeking, but Charlie is better at hiding."

"You're right," giggled Brutus. "Charlie is not even playing yet and he is winning."

"I have not seen him today. Did you look in the barn?" The cat purred.

"We have not looked there yet; we will go there next." said Scrump.

"Thank you," said Brutus as they walked back down the steps.

They went to the barn next. They did not find Charlie but found a little white mouse. "Excuse us, Mrs. Mouse," said Scrump politely. "We are looking for our friend Charlie. He is a small grey squirrel with a poofy tail and a little pink nose."

"I have not seen him today," said the mouse. "If I do, I will let him know you are looking for him."

"Thank you very much," said Brutus. "I hope you have a good day."

Brutus Loses His Sniffer

Since Charlie was not in the barn, Brutus and Scrump went out to the big tree next to the barn. This was where they had first met Charlie. They sat outside of Scrump's burrow and called up into the big oak tree.

A little grey head poked out from behind some leaves. "Hi, I'm Charlie's little sister, Colleen. He is not here right now, but he said if you guys come looking for him to tell you that he is by the edge of the woods helping Mom."

"Ok, thanks, Colleen!" said Scrump.

"We will see if we can find him," added Brutus.

Brutus Loses His Sniffer

They raced away from the big oak tree and around the back of the barn to the fence at the edge of the woods. "Charlie," they called as they walked along the fence.

"Over here past the big rock!" Charlie called back. Brutus and Scrump started running toward the sound and passed the big rock. They finally saw Charlie hanging upside down on a tree trunk.

"Hi, Charlie." greeted Scrump. "Your sister told us you would be at the edge of the woods."

"We were going to play hide and seek today. Do you want to play today?" asked Brutus.

"I can't today. I have to help my mom collect straw and fluff for the nest," explained Charlie.

"What do you use straw and fluff for?" Brutus asked.

"It helps keep the drey warm in the winter. Our nests are called dreys, they are built out of sticks and leaves and then we have to put in soft and warm stuff like straw, feathers, fur and even fluff that we find in the cotton fields or from the humans' pillows they leave on the porch," explained Charlie.

"Oh, that makes sense. I never knew that squirrel nests had so much inside them," said Brutus.

"Yeah, thanks for telling us," Scrump agreed. "We will let you get back to work then, but maybe you can play tomorrow?"

Brutus and Scrump walked back to the middle of the clover field.

"Well, I guess since Charlie can't play today, that means you're it," said Scrump.

Brutus laid down and put his paws over his eyes and started to count.

Scrump zig-zagged through the clover field and around the pond. Then he squeezed under the garden fence.

Brutus was still counting.

Scrump ran around the garden, scooting under and around bushes and vegetables. He ran out of the garden gate and to the playground.

Brutus was taking a long time to count.

Scrump ran around the tree with the tire swing, then jumped over a fallen log. He went up the steps to the top of the slide and looked around for a place to hide. From way up there he could see so many places. There was a thicket of tall grass and cattails next to the pond. There was a big pile of leaves near the fence by the woods. Past the pond, he could see a tree laying down with some of the roots pointing up.

Scrump thought quickly about each spot and decided against them. He continued to look around and finally he saw the perfect place to hide. Down he slid and landed with a thud, then he bounded off to the place he had seen.

Brutus finished counting and called out, "Apple, Peaches, Pumpkin Pie. Ready or not, holler I!"

He waited a minute but did not hear a response from Scrump. He put his nose to the ground and found his friend's rabbity smell. He zig-zagged through the clover field and around the pond. He squeezed under the garden fence and around the vegetables. He sniffed his way out of the garden and to the tire swing, over the log and up the slide.

At the top of the slide, he stopped sniffing and looked around. He could not see Scrump anywhere from there. Down the slide he slid, landing with a bump. He sniffed the ground and found his friend's smell. With his nose to the ground, he followed the smell to the flower beds. It was in the flowers that he felt a sharp pain in on his nose and lost Scrump's scent.

With his eyes blurry and watering from the sharp sting, Brutus looked around the flowers, but he could not see Scrump. He perked up his ears and listened, but the only thing he heard was the buzz of bees. He went around in circles with his nose to the ground, trying to find his friend's scent.

Scrump watched Brutus from his hiding place. He had to bite his tongue to keep himself from laughing. Brutus always found him super-fast. He really had found a good hiding place this time.

Brutus Loses His Sniffer

Brutus closed his eyes and walked around and around with his nose to the ground, sniffing and sniffing as hard as he could. Then he yelped, walking around with his nose on the ground and his eyes closed was not a good idea. He wasn't looking where he was going and ran nose-first into a big, hard rock. Brutus shook his head in pain and tried to smell again. His nose felt big and stuffy, and it hurt to sniff. Sadly, he went back to the slide where he had last smelled his friend. He went to the top and looked around again. He could not see his friend and his nose really hurt.

At the top of the slide, he sat and started to cry. After a few minutes, he heard a small voice behind him ask, "Why are you up here crying? Are you afraid to slide?"

"No," whined Brutus not looking up. "I lost my sniffer, and I can't find my friend Scrump."

"How did you lose your sniffer and Scrump?" the animal asked.

"We were playing hide and seek, I followed Scrump's smell up and down the slide. When I got to the flowers, I couldn't smell him anymore. Then I hit my nose on a rock and now I can't smell anything."

Brutus Loses His Sniffer

"Oh, I see!" said the animal. "My name is Patches. I can't help you with your sniffer, but I will help you find your friend." She slid down the slide, leaving Brutus to follow her.

It took a moment, but Brutus decided that sulking wasn't going to help. He slid down and followed Patches.

Brutus Loses His Sniffer

Together, Brutus and Patches went back to the flower beds. They crawled under a big rose bush, and around many flower bushes. They went around and between every plant in the flower garden. Finally in the corner near the end of the flower garden, they found Scrump. He was curled up tight against the base of a lilac bush whose branches almost touched the ground, hiding the bush's trunk. There, they found Scrump sound asleep.

"What took you so long?" Scrump asked with a yawn.

Brutus told him all about smelling him in the clovers and around the pond, under the fence and over the log, up the steps and down the slide. Then Brutus started to cry again, "When I passed the biggest rose bush, I bonked my nose and lost my sniffer." Brutus whined.

"This is Patches," Brutus said nodding at the black and white fuzzy animal next to him. "She found me when I went back to the slide and offered to help me find you. She is good at finding people."

Just then Brutus heard a strange rattle noise behind him. He jumped and turned around just in time to see a small head with beady little eyes and a long neck in front of him. The snake opened his mouth and Brutus saw two very sharp looking fangs. Scrump and Brutus both jumped and tried to back away.

Patches jumped, too, but then she turned her back toward the snake. She stuck her tail up in the air and fluffed up her fur.

The snake turned around and slithered quickly away.

"Wow, that was close!" exclaimed Scrump.

"Yeah," said Brutus, "But what is that smell?"

"The smell is me," said Patches, "That's what I do when I get scared. Wait, you can smell it? I thought you lost your sniffer?"

"Hey, yeah, I did," said Brutus, "I guess you helped me find Scrump and my sniffer. Thank you!" He laughed.

"So, do you guys want to play more hide and seek?" asked Scrump.

"Most people do not want to play with me after I do that," Patches stated sadly with her head down.

"We will," said Brutus. "But maybe we should make a rule that the seeker can only seek with their eyes, not their noses."

They all laughed.

Scrump laid down, covered his eyes, and began to count.

ABOUT THE AUTHOR

Tif E. Boots wrote her first children's book as a birthday present for her daughter. Many years later it has been shared with her sister, cousins, classmates, and now you. Tif was raised in Marana, Arizona and was working concession stands at county fairs in Arizona and Michigan with her family until she graduated from Marana High School in 2000. She became a mother and correctional officer in 2004. She then moved to Nevada, Missouri with her family where she was blessed with her second daughter and fell into a career of nurse's assistant for Hospice. Tif and her family relocated to Mulberry, Florida in 2017. In her free time, Tif can usually be found on the water or at amusement parks spending time with family and friends, and simply enjoying the life that God has blessed her with.

ABOUT THE ILLUSTRATOR

Syranity Barker is an illustrator who has always had a love for art. She was born in Tucson, Arizona and eventually moved to central Florida where she graduated high school. Syranity illustrated her love of drawing early in life; her family were great supporters of her passions and always made sure she had a variety of supplies and mediums. While she was still in high school, her work was entered in numerous art shows. She received the City Commissioners Choice Award for a mixed media portrait of her dog and has sold several pieces of her work. Still fresh out of high school, Syranity works two jobs and illustrates professionally in her spare time. She is currently the in-house illustrator for ShelteringTree.Earth Publishing and also promotes herself as a free-lance artist. Syranity enjoys singing, skating, spending time with her friends and family, and creating her own characters and writing backstories for them. Syranity aspires to become an art teacher and share her passion for drawing and self-expression with others.

GUIDE FOR SMALL GROUPS, CLASSES, AND INDIVIDUAL REFLECTION

DIRECTIONS: Write or draw your answers in the space below the question.

1. What is Scrump doing when Brutus finds him?

2. What makes Scrump stop what he is doing and prepare to run?

3. Where is Charlie today?

4. Who told them where to find him?

5. Why can't he play hide and seek with them?

6. Name 3 things that are used to make a drey.

7. Where does Scrump go after leaving the clover field?

8. Why do you think Brutus lost the scent before he bumped his nose?

9. Where would you hide?

10. Is it fair that Brutus uses his nose to search for Scrump?

11. Why do you think Scrump did not hide in the tall grass by the pond?

12. Do you think the fallen tree would have made a good hiding place?

13. Do you think the big pile of leaves would make a good place to hide?

14. Who found Brutus at the top of the slide?

15. What was Brutus doing when Patches found him?

16. Where do they go to look for Scrump?

17. What was Scrump doing when they found him?

18. What was behind Brutus when he heard the strange rattle sound?

19. What did Patches do that scared the snake away?

20. What caused Brutus to find his sniffer again?

21. Why don't most people play with Patches?

22. Why do they add a new rule to the game?

For more information,
to become one of our authors,
translators, or illustrators,
or to contact the author or illustrator:

ShelteringTreeMedia.com